My Baby Brother IS a Little Monster

By Sarah Albee
Illustrated by Tom Brannon

Creative Edge, 2007. All rights reserved.
Published by Creative Edge, 2007, an imprint of Dalmatian Press, LLC, Franklin, Tennessee 37067. No part of this book

Printed in China
ISBN: 1-40378-101-X

07 08 09 10 GUA 10 9 8 7 6 5 4 3 2 1
CE10178 Sesame Street 8x8 Storybook: My Baby Brother is a Little Monster

"Hi, Henry," said Big Bird. "Ready to go to the park?"

"I'm ready," replied Henry. "But my mom can't take us until my brother wakes up from his nap."

"Oh, okay," said Big Bird.

Henry sighed. "We have to play inside until he's ready."

"Nice to see you, Big Bird," said Henry's mother. "Calvin should be awake soon."

Just then, Big Bird heard a horrible noise. "Wow! What's that?" he said.

Henry rolled his eyes. "That's my brother. He's awake."

"Big Bird," said Henry, "meet Calvin."
Big Bird smiled at Calvin.
Calvin drooled and blew bubbles.

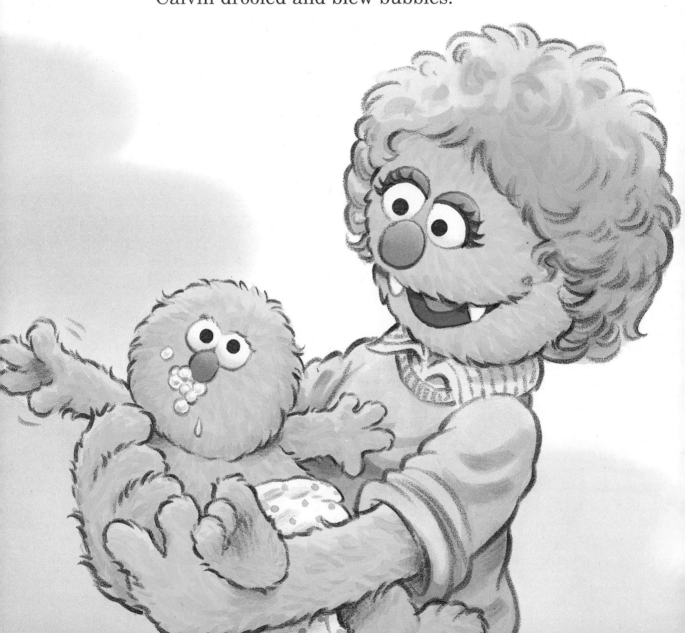

"Can we go to the park now?" Henry asked.
"In a few minutes," said Henry's mother.

While his mother was making Calvin's cereal, Calvin crawled over and knocked down Henry and Big Bird's block castle.

"Gee," said Big Bird. "You want to play a game or something?"

"Mom, *now* can we go to the park?" asked Henry.

"Pretty soon, honey," replied his mother. "Oh, isn't your brother adorable? Let me take a picture of the two of you together."

"Ouch!" said Henry.
"Why don't you tell him not to do that?" asked Big Bird.
"He doesn't understand that it hurts," replied Henry.
"He's just a *little* monster."

"*Eeeew!* Mom!" called Henry, holding his nose. "Calvin needs to be changed!"

Henry's mother carried Calvin away to change his diaper.

"I wish you'd hurry up and eat that!" Henry told his brother. SPLAT! Calvin decided he was finished with his lunch. "Wow," said Big Bird. "Your baby brother sure is messy."

Henry had had enough. "I'm sick of having a baby around! He makes dumb baby noises and he messes up my toys and he throws food around. I wish," said Henry, his lip starting to tremble, "I wish I didn't have a baby brother!"

Henry's mother gave Henry a big hug. "Sweetie, I know it can be hard to have a little brother. It's okay to feel angry with him sometimes. Calvin is lucky to have such a patient big brother."

"Really?" said Henry, wiping his eyes.

"Come on! Let's go to the park!" said his mother.

A little while later, as they were playing catch, Big Bird stopped. "Hey, Henry," he said softly, "I think Calvin just said your name."

Henry hurried over to Calvin. "Mom!" he shrieked. "Hey, Mom! Calvin said my name!"

Henry's mother ran over to listen, too.

"En-wee, En-wee," Calvin said.